Rosa Rose

Rosa Rose

AND OTHER POEMS BY

Robert Priest

ILLUSTRATED BY
Joan Krygsman

WOLSAK
& WYNN

Cover image: Joan Krygsman
Cover and interior design: Marijke Friesen
Author photograph: Allen Booth
Typeset in Celeste
Printed by Coach House Printing Company Toronto, Canada

The Canada Council | Le Conseil des Arts
for the Arts | du Canada

ONTARIO ARTS COUNCIL
CONSEIL DES ARTS DE L'ONTARIO
50 YEARS OF ONTARIO GOVERNMENT SUPPORT OF THE ARTS
50 ANS DE SOUTIEN DU GOUVERNEMENT DE L'ONTARIO AUX ARTS

Canadian   Patrimoine
Heritage   canadien

The publisher gratefully acknowledges the support of the Canada
Council for the Arts, the Ontario Arts Council and the Canada Book Fund.

The author would like to acknowledge and thank the people of Canada for
the generous support given through The Canada Council for the Arts and
The Ontario Arts Council.

Wolsak and Wynn Publishers Ltd.
280 James Street North
Hamilton, ON
Canada L8R 2L3

Library and Archives Canada Cataloguing in Publication

Priest, Robert, 1951–
        Rosa Rose / Robert Priest; illustrated by Joan Krygsman.

Poems.
ISBN 978-1-894987-73-8

        1. Role models–Juvenile poetry. 2. Children's poetry,
Canadian (English). I. Krygsman, Joan Margret II. Title.

PS8581.R47R68 2013   jC811'.54   C2013-901091-2

TABLE OF CONTENTS

ROSA SAT

Rosa sat, she sat on the bus,
She sat with a weary smile.
The driver said she must get up
For a white man stood in the aisle.

But she refused, she refused,
She stayed in the seat she chose.
She sat until the sheriff came
And only then she rose.

Rosa rose, Rosa rose,
She'd sooner be arrested
Than obey an unjust law
That law would now be tested.

Rosa rose, and the people rose
She went to court and she won.
Rosa rose and the people rose
And they'd only just begun.

TERRY RAN

Terry ran, Terry ran,
  He strode from hip to heel.
    One leg was muscle, bone and skin,
      One fibreglass and steel.

Across the land from Newfoundland
  Where highways stream and slope,
    Twenty-three miles a day he ran
      On his Marathon of Hope.

One will to drive that young man on,
  One heart to make it real,
    One leg of muscle, bone and skin,
      One fibreglass and steel.

Terry ran, he ran through pain,
  He laughed and he endured
    Raising money every step
      So cancer could be cured.

One hope to help to find a cure,
  One quest to make it pay.
    He inspired the whole wide world,
      Raised millions on the way.

Terry ran, Terry ran,
  He strode from hip to heel.
    One leg was muscle, bone and skin,
      One fibreglass and steel.

GANDHI WALKED

To the sea
To the sea for salt
To the sea where salt is made
Gandhi walked to the sea for salt,
The salt the law forbade

For just a taste
For just a taste of salt
For just a taste of salt he prayed
Gandhi walked to the sea for salt
And he was unafraid

They shouted, "*Stop!*"
They shouted, "*Halt!*"
But Gandhi disobeyed
Thousands joined the march for salt
A great big long parade

Two hundred miles
Two hundred miles they walked
Two hundred miles through sun and shade
All the way to the sea for salt,
The sea where salt is made

They shouted, "*Stop!*"
They shouted, "*Halt!*"
But Gandhi disobeyed
He boiled sea water in a pot
And when the salt was made
He took a single taste

11

With just a taste
With just a taste of salt
With just a taste was freedom made
All the marchers then made salt
The salt the law forbade
And they all took a taste
And they were unafraid

And so the law was changed.

GANDHI WALKED TO DANDI

Gandhi walked to Dandi,
To Dandi Gandhi walked.
Gandhi walked to Dandi
To get a pinch of salt.

Gandhi got to Dandi,
To Dandi Gandhi got.
The sea was salt and sandy;
Gandhi poured some in a pot.

He boiled off all the water
In Dandi by the sea,
And so he made some sea salt
For his special recipe.

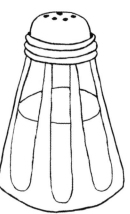

To make delicious
All the dishes
Of people's wishes
For freedom.

He was a very gentle man,
A slow and steady stepper.
For salt he brought the empire down –
What if he'd wanted pepper?

LOUIS HAD A HORN

Jazz was in the air
Just waiting to be born
And Louis had something –
Louis had a horn.

LOUIS PLAYED

He was –
A son of a son of a slave,
He was raised by a single mom.
He was partying New Year's Eve,
When Louis fired off a gun.
Just in celebration
Just for the bang and the glory
But Louis was charged by police
And sent to reformatory.
(Poor Louis, poor Louis! Just twelve years old
When he went to reformatory.)

He was –
A child of a child of the street,
In Storyville Louis was born.
When the prison band took up the beat
Louis took up the horn.
What an amazing sensation!
What a big blast of glory!
Soon he was best in the band,
The best in reformatory.
(Yes Louis, O Louis, was just thirteen,
And the best in reformatory.)

It was –
The hub of the hub of the world,
The scene of all musical scenes,
When Louis was finally set free
In Storyville, New Orleans.

He hit the streets a blastin',
No gun but a cornet in hand,
King Oliver heard him play
And asked him to join his band.
(O Louis, O Louis was just fourteen
When he joined King Oliver's band.)

There's a –
C above C above high C
It's an almost impossible note,
which Louis was able to play
Two hundred times in a row
Just in competition;
He sure made the blues sound pretty.
Soon he could solo all night,
Soon he was best in the city.
(O Louis, O Louis, he was just fifteen
And he was best in the city.)

There was –
A dream of a dream of music
That hadn't quite got there yet
Some say it finally arrived
When Louis took up his cornet.
If any can play it better
Nobody ever has –
Louis changed music forever, they say,
The king of the kings of jazz.

DEEPA MADE

She made a film called *Fire*
And a second film called *Earth*
Both were about India
The land of her birth.
Many people loved them
Though all did not agree
When she returned to India
For film number three.

Water *she would call it,*
One and two and three –
Fire, Earth *and* Water –
Deepa's trilogy.

She'd tell a tale of widows
Their strength and misery
Deserted and abandoned
To live in poverty.
Deepa chose the actors
Millions were invested
But when she built her first set
A local group protested.

They didn't like her story
Which Deepa said was strange
They hadn't even read it
No way she'd make a change!
Deepa shot her first scene
Where River Ganges churned
The group came in the dark of night
And the whole set was burned.

She tried to shoot the movie
In other Indian towns
But every place refused her
Her permits were turned down.
Her life was even threatened
And the funding was withdrawn
People said she should give up
"No way you can go on."

Back she went to Canada,
She started out from scratch
It took her four more years of toil
Before she raised the cash
And still she'd need that permit
She tried and tried and tried
But every town turned Deepa down
Permission was denied.

So she took on a different film
She'd call it *River Moon*
And shoot it in Sri Lanka
With a different cast and crew.
Had Deepa finally given in,
Her story left untold?
Deepa called out "Action Please"
And the cameras rolled

And told a tale of widows
Who lived in poverty
Fire, Earth and ... *River Moon?*
Ah ... Deepa's trickery!
Yes, Deepa Mehta made her film,
No, she was not defeated,
She told the tale of a widow child
And how she was mistreated.

A film she then called *Water.*
One and two and three –
Fire, **Earth** *and* **Water** –
Deepa's trilogy.

SAPPHO WROTE

We're putting Sappho together again
    Piece by precious piece;
Her verses are coming together again,
    This poet of ancient Greece.

She was the poet of people in love,
    The bard of joy and tears,
Her songs were sung by old and young
    And known for a thousand years.

Scrolls of papyrus don't age very well,
    Water and wind and fire
Will do their worst even to verse
    That sings of love and desire.

Books that survived such trials of time
    And live on to this day
Were scribed by monks who copied them
    Before they could decay.

They saved the works they loved the best
    In praise of God above
But what monks blessed and loved the best
    Weren't songs of human love.

So Sappho's poetry dwindled away,
    Slowly it disappeared –
Sappho was lost and remained that way
    Almost a thousand years.

But now archaeology's bringing her back
    From so many ancient hands
That quoted her lines in love letters found
    Preserved in dry desert sands;

Lyrical poems so moving and true
    They just had to write them down,
Assembled from fragments scattered in heaps
    Or buried in tombs underground.

We're putting Sappho together again
    Piece by precious piece;
Her verses are coming together again
    This poet of ancient Greece.

Lovers have saved her – the poet of love
    She was lost beyond recall.
Sappho of Lesbos, we love your lines!
    One day we'll have them all.

ALI WOULDN'T FIGHT

Ali was the champ
Bam! Bam! Bam!
The best boxer ever
And man, could he dance.
Plus he was a joker
And he spouted poetry.
He was born Cassius Clay
But became Ali –
Muhammad Ali.
He laughed and he twirled.
He was the *Bam! Bam! Bam!*
Heavyweight champion
Of the world.

Now in those days
Blam! Blam! Blam!
There was a war
In Vietnam.
Blam! Blam! Blam!
It was a terrible war,
A terrible war in Vietnam.

And when they called
Ali to go
He refused,
He just said, "No,
I think I'll stay here
Where I am,
I've got no quarrel
With Vietnam.
Why would I kill
My fellow man?"

If you don't fight
Blam! Blam! Blam!
You'll go to jail
Wham! Wham! Wham!
If you don't fight
For Uncle Sam,
We'll lock you up
In the *slam, slam, slam.*
But he wouldn't fight
Blam! Blam! Blam!
He just said no
To Uncle Sam.
"I think I'll stay here,
Where I am,
I've got no quarrel
With Vietnam.
I'm a recent convert
To Islam.
Why would I kill
My fellow man?"

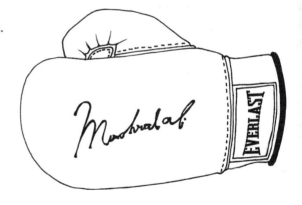

Ali was charged
But he wouldn't budge.
He was put on trial
Before a judge.
The gavel came down
Wham! Wham! Wham!
Ali was free,
An innocent man,
He didn't have to fight
In Vietnam,
He didn't have to fight
For Uncle Sam.

But he still couldn't box
Bam! Bam! Bam!
They wouldn't let him box
And they picked a new champ
And still there was a war
Blam! Blam! Blam!
And many people died
In Vietnam.

Ali had to wait,
This champ of the world,
Down by his sides
Those big fists curled,
Not till the war
Came at last to an end
Would they let him fight
For the prize again.
Back in the ring
How good Ali felt
When he fought George Foreman
And took back his belt.
He darted and danced,
Spoke poetry and twirled.
He was the king of *not* fighting
And the heavyweight champion
Of the world.

Yes, he was champ in the ring
And a champ times two –
Cause Ali was the king
Of *not* fighting too!

THE MAN WHO STOPPED TANKS

The tanks were rolling fast
To Tiananmen Square,
Heading for the protesters
To get them out of there.

Along came a man,
Two shopping bags in hand,
He turned to face a tank
And there he took a stand.

The tank kept rolling
As though it might kill.
He stood there steady;
He remained still.

He was not some soldier
With a weapon in his fist,
He risked his very life
Standing there like this.

The tank rolled closer,
It wouldn't be blocked,
But two feet away
It suddenly stopped.

First one tank
Then the tank behind,
Three, four, five tanks
All stopped in a line.

There the tanks stood
While the tension grew;
They turned to go around him
But he stood there too.

He looked so ordinary
So young and so thin.
The tanks didn't move
What was stopping them?

They were under orders.
What force held them there?
Two blocks away
From Tiananmen Square.

The man was dragged away
By two people in the end.
But were they policemen
Or were they his friends?

What was his name?
Nobody knows.
What happened to him?
Where did he go?

The man who stopped tanks,
Is he here or there?
You no longer see him
In Tiananmen Square.

You no longer see him
Anywhere –
It's like he has vanished
Into thin air.

Some say he's jailed,
Others say he's dead.
He might be in Taiwan
Or hiding in Tibet.

O man who stopped tanks
We think of you and wonder
What was your superpower?
What spell where they under?

FOR WHAT THEY DID AND DIDN'T DO

To the man who stood still
And the man who didn't kill
For what they did
And didn't do with tanks
I'd like to offer my thanks.

ELIJAH HELD A FEATHER

"What power has an eagle feather?"
The teacher asked the child.
"It has no power on its own
Like eagles in the wild

"It cannot fly, it hardly floats,
It wafts down to the ground."
Elijah let the priest drone on;
He didn't make a sound.

He just held that eagle feather
Lightly in his hand
And thought of home and family,
His people and the land.

He was a child so far from home
In a residential school
Where treatment of First Nations' kids
Was often very cruel

O yes, he suffered words and blows
And much else that was wrong,
Perhaps the eagle feather was
What kept Elijah strong

For he grew up and he returned
To home and family
And with that feather he became
A chief among the Cree.

Next he ran for Parliament
They said he could not win
No native ever had before
But he was voted in.

Then one day Mulroney tried
To fix the Constitution:
Special treatment for Quebec,
That was his solution.

First Nations when they heard the news
Were angry and insulted;
Their native rights weren't guaranteed.
Why weren't they consulted?

Despite their wrath Mulroney said,
*"That's how it has to be
The deal is done. Finis, my friends, –*
A fait accompli."

There was a hitch though in his plan,
A glitch he did not see,
There'd be a vote across the land
Each province must agree

And one by one they all said, *"Yes,
Let's do this deal together,"*
But when Elijah stood to vote
He held that eagle feather.

"*No*," Elijah Harper said,
This man of so few words.
For native people he said, "*No*"
Till then they'd gone unheard.

He held the floor and spoke his mind
And he could not be stopped
He spoke until the deadline passed
And so the deal was blocked.

What power has an eagle feather?
People gather round!
Elijah and that eagle feather
Brought Mulroney down.

He just held that eagle feather
Lightly in his hand
And thought of home and family,
His people and the land.

ELIJAH HARPER'S FILIBUSTER

All Mulroney's
Gall and bluster
Couldn't shush
Or even fluster
Elijah Harper's filibuster.

CHASING EINSTEIN 'ROUND THE TABLE AT LIGHTSPEED

                thesis)   The   faster

     Albert's   Albert's

   that's   father

least   runs

(At   The

large   more

infinitely   his

    grows   mass

        he   increases

             Till

WANGARI PLANTED A TREE

Wangari Maathai
Slowly bent down
And planted seven seedlings
In the dry Kenyan ground.
They said, *"Women can't!"*
She said, *"Anyone can!"*
She planted seven seedlings,
So it began.

Wangari Maathai
Started going round
Teaching girls and women
To plant seedlings in the ground.
"Who says women can't?"
She said, *"Anyone can."*
They planted seeds and seedlings
In the dry Kenyan land.

Village by village those seedlings grew
And the branches spread and green leaves, too.
And there were more and more trees, more nuts and fruits,
More soil held together by more and more roots.
And the water that would've run away stayed
And the tree frogs chattered and the children played
While the trees stretched out their cool green shade
From village to village in one decade.
What a belt Wangari and her women made
All across Kenya and then way beyond –
All round the world people carried it on.

Wangari Maathai,
We're down on our knees,
We're going to thank you
By planting more trees.
Greenbelts of forest
Across every land,
If they say, "*People can't,*"
We'll say, "*People can!*"

Women of Kenya,
You lift your gaze high
To green leaves a-waving
Way up in the sky.
Young girls of Kenya,
We sing praise to you.
If they say, "*People can't,*"
We'll say, "*Look – People do!*"

GREENBELT SONG

What kind of belt –
O tell me please –
Holds up the sky
On a river of leaves?

A belt made of forest
A greenbelt of trees
Can hold up the sky
On a river of leaves.

What kind of belt –
I'll ask you again –
Can hold up the tree frogs
The nuts and the grain?

To hold up the tree frogs,
The nuts and the grain,
To hold up the soil
The sun and the rain

You need a greenbelt
A green canopy
You need a greenbelt
Woven from trees.

What kind of belt –
Has anyone heard –
Can hold high the monkeys
The bees and the birds?

To hold high the monkeys
The bees and the birds
To hold up the river
Bring water to herds

We need a greenbelt
A green flag unfurled
A greenbelt right round
The waist of the world.

JULIA BUTTERFLY HILL

Julia Butterfly Hill
She climbed a redwood tree
She wouldn't come down until
The lumberjacks agreed

To save that tree, that ancient tree
And the grove where it had grown
Eighteen hundred summers of sun
Upon a ridge of stone.

They tried to take her down
They tried to shake her down
They even cut her food supply
To break her down

But Julia Butterfly Hill
She stayed there way up high
Through heat and winter's chill
Until a year passed by

Up in that tree, that ancient tree
And the grove where it had grown
Eighteen hundred autumns of rain
Up on that ridge of stone.

They tried to wear her down
They tried to tear her down
They put a chopper in the air
To scare her down

But Julia butterfly Hill
Two years in sun and wind
They could not break her will
So finally they gave in

And spared that tree, that ancient tree
And the grove where it had grown
Eighteen hundred winters of wind
Upon that ridge of stone.

Julia Butterfly Hill
slowly she came down
the grove was safe and still
she wept and kissed the ground.

A TREE WILL TAKE THE HEAT FOR YOU

A
Tree will take
The heat for you
When shelter can't be found
When the sun is bearing down
In a great hot force that staggers you
A tree casts a cool shade – almost liquid –
As you walk along two hundred feet beneath
The lowest, singing leaf.
A tree will take the wind for you, bending into it
From far away so all you hear is rustling
And the creak of wooden limbs as you lean against it – safe.
A tree will take the rain for you
And roll it round in a riverbed of living leaves high overhead.
A tree will stand by you in all kinds of weather
And even when you're lonely
A tree will hold the earth still
In its green grip
So you can climb into
its arms
and be
held there
in creature
music
with bugs
and birds
unafraid –
part of the
music now,
part of the shade.

WELL WELL

if you place
the well well
and you dig
the well well
and you treat
the well well
the water in
the well will be
well well well
& if the water
in the well is
well well well
the well itself
is well as well.
It's a well well.
And a well well
keeps the people
who drink from
the well well as well.
Well, well, well! Well, well, well! Treat your well well; keep your well well.

LULU THE POT-BELLIED PIG

Down by the lake
In a mobile home,
A woman named Jo Ann
Was sitting on her own
Except for her dog,
An Eskimo dog,
And her pet pig,
A pot-bellied pig,
Lulu, the pot-bellied pig.

"Oh!" Jo Ann gasped,
She let out a moan.
Jo Ann called, "Help!"
But she was all alone.
The dog looked scared.
No one else was there
Except for the pig,
Her pet pig,
Lulu, the pot-bellied pig.

She clutched her chest
And fell like a stone,
Her second heart attack
And she didn't have a phone.
The dog just yelped
But who was gonna help
Other than her pig,
Her pet pig,
Lulu, the pot-bellied pig?

Lulu looked around
She had to get out.
There – the doggy door,
She pushed with her snout.
She was so big
The door so small
But she squeezed herself in
And started to crawl.
It scraped her belly,
She thought she'd explode,
But she wriggled on through
And ran to the road.

Off in the distance
Cars were coming fast.
How could she stop them
From zooming right past?
She waddled to the middle
Of the road and flopped;
Down to her pot-bellied
Belly she dropped!
Cars wheeled around her
Cars peeled around,
Cars squealed around her
Until one stopped
And from that car
A young man popped.

Lulu stood up,
Her snout showed the way,
She led him to her home
Where Jo Ann still lay.
An ambulance was called
In time it arrived –
Fifteen minutes more
And Jo Ann would have died.
But Jo Ann survived.
Jo Ann is alive

Thanks to her pig,
Her pet pig:
Lulu the life-saving
Pot-bellied pig!

THE PEACE OF MANY PIECES

Peace be upon you and under your feet.
Peace be before you like the wind before the wheat.
Peace be within you, yes a peace so sweet
Is a peace of many pieces; let it be complete.

Peace be upon you and peace be below,
Peace upon the mountains and the fields of snow.
Peace upon the people living in the street,
It's a peace of many pieces; let it be complete.

Your peace and my peace are good together.

Peace be upon you – compassionate peace,
Peace upon the anguished and the so-called least.
Peace upon the children and the birds and beasts,
It's a piece of many pieces; let it be complete.

Your peace and my peace, they fit together.

Peace be upon you and peace be below,
Peace upon the mountains and the fields of snow.
Peace upon the table, let the hunger cease.
It's a peace of many pieces; let it be complete.

Your peace and my peace, they fit together.
Your peace and my peace, they're good together,
They work together.

MY MOTHER HAS MILLIONS OF MOTHERS

My mother has millions of mothers
  It took millions of mothers to make her
    Mothers who became grandmothers
      Mothers who became great-grandmothers
        Of great-great-grandmothers
      And on and on
    Great rivers of mothers flow
  Into every mother
And in every mother's hands
  Millions of hands move again, soothe again
    Mothers who care, mothers who teach
      Mothers who feed, who watch over you
        Encouraging you
      Mothers of daughters
    Who grow up to have daughters
  Who are mothers of sons
Who grow up to be fathers
  And grandfathers
    And great-grandfathers
      Of great-great-grandfathers
      And on and on
        It took millions of fathers to make my father
      Millions of hands flow into his hands
As he lifts me up to his shoulders
  Your father is huge with fathers
    Your mother is grand with mothers
      With ancestors
        It's true
      Millions of fathers and mothers
  Made your father and mother
Made you

TILL THE END'S END'S END

My mother's mother's mother
Was my great-grandma.
My brother's mother's husband
Was my dear old pa.

My neighbour's neighbour's neighbour
Is my friend's friend's friend.
We're all in it together,
Till the end's end's end.

Great-Granddad's daughter's daughter
Is my dad's wife, ma.
My brother's lawyer's lawyer,
Is my brother-in-law.

My homie's homie's homie
Is my friend's friend's friend.
We're all in it together,
Till the end's end's end.

And O, my son's son's sons,
No one owns the sun.
O my daughter's daughter's daughters,
The water is everyone's.

My buddy's buddy's buddy
Il est mon ami.
My sister's brother's brother
Is my mom's son – me

My rabbi's doctor's nephew,
Is my sister's best friend.
We're all in this together,
Till it all starts up again.

We're all in this together,
Till the end's end's end.

ACKNOWLEDGEMENTS

For their helpful editing suggestions on some of these poems I would like to thank Allen Booth, Susan Glickman and Ashley Hisson. I'm also grateful to those who came before: Mother Goose, Cicely Mary Barker, Edward Lear, Dr. Seuss, Dennis Lee and Shel Silverstein. And thanks to my sons, Eli and Daniel Kirzner-Priest.

NOTES ON THE POEMS

I wrote these poems to celebrate some of the people whose achievements have inspired me in my life. I've known many of these stories for a long time but some of them I only encountered during the writing of this book. There are many more inspiring people out there. To them I say, "Thank you!"

MUHAMMAD ALI (1942–), known to many as "The Greatest," was an Olympic boxing champ in his late teens. He was heavyweight champion three different times between 1965 and 1979 and often promoted his matches by taunting his opponents with rhyming dancing poems that many people say were an inspiration for hip hop. During the Vietnam War he refused to serve in the US army, stating it was against his personal and religious beliefs. It is estimated that over five million civilians and military personnel died between 1959–1975 in the Vietnam War.

LOUIS ARMSTRONG (1901–1971) went on to become the best-known jazz trumpet player of all time. He wrote and recorded so many songs, and sold so many millions of records worldwide it is difficult to find accurate figures. He was also a beloved singer whose style continues to influence singers and composers long after his death. The generous King Oliver, one of Louis's many mentors, was a renowned jazz trumpeter and soloist in his own right.

ALBERT EINSTEIN (1879–1955) is widely regarded as the most influential scientist of the twentieth century. At the age of twenty-six he revolutionized physics with his Special Theory of Relativity. Albert's theory, which is summed up in the famous equation $E=mc^2$, stated that the closer anything moves to the speed of light the greater its mass becomes until it becomes infinitely large. As far as I know Albert's father never did chase him around the table at lightspeed but if he had...

TERRY FOX (1958–1981) was a Canadian athlete who lost a leg to cancer. Cross-country runs in Terry's honour are still conducted every year, continuing to raise money for Terry's chosen cause: research into and prevention of cancer.

MOHANDAS GANDHI (1869–1948), known as the "Mahatma" or "great soul," believed in bringing about change by non-violent means such as non-cooperation, boycotts, strikes and civil disobedience. At the time, India was under the rule of Britain, whose parliament had forbidden Indians to make their own salt because they wanted Indians to buy it from them. The Salt March which is featured in this poem drew worldwide attention. Dandi is the name of the town on the sea coast where the Salt March arrived. After many years of struggle, Gandhi's tactics succeeded and India achieved its independence in 1948.

ELIJAH HARPER (1949–) served as a member of Alberta's legislative assembly where he became the minister of northern affairs. Brian Mulroney was the prime minister of Canada at the time. The deal he had made, known as the Meech

Lake Accord, needed to be passed by June 23, 1990. The tactic of blocking a passage of legislation by prolonged speaking until its deadline has passed is known as a "filibuster." Not long after Elijah Harper's filibuster, Brian Mulroney resigned as prime minister. Elijah Harper is still active in issues of social justice.

JULIA "BUTTERFLY" HILL (1974–) got her nickname "Butterfly" as a child when a butterfly landed on her finger and stayed there for hours. The California redwood tree she sat in for two years is fifty-five metres tall. She did it to prevent the Pacific Lumber Company from cutting it down. She had an eight-person support team who hoisted supplies up and down from the ground to the top of the tree. As a result of her act of civil disobedience, she saved not only the tree she sat in but all the trees for two hundred metres around it.

As far as I've been able to ascertain, **JO ANN** and **LULU**, her pet pig, are still alive and thriving, as is the dog.

WANGARI MAATHAI's (1940–2011) victories were not easily won. She suffered beatings and even jail time for her actions. Eventually her achievements were recognized and she was elected Member of Parliament. She founded the Green Belt Movement, and won the Nobel Peace Prize in 2000 for her work on behalf of the environment, democracy and women's rights.

THE MAN WHO STOPPED TANKS. The image referred to in this poem of a man standing in front of tanks is one of the most famous photographs in history. At the time it was taken, a huge number of people had been occupying Tiananmen Square in the centre of Beijing in a mass movement aimed at bringing about democratic reform in China. Unfortunately the man's courage only delayed the tanks. Eventually many other tanks and soldiers made their way to the square and the protest was brutally crushed.

DEEPA MEHTA (1950–) is an Indo-Canadian filmmaker. The film *Water*, the making of which is described in the poem, reached a vast audience and was nominated for an Academy award. Her latest film is *Midnight's Children.* For more information about the making of the film, and a good story too, I recommend the book *Shooting Water: A Mother-Daughter Journey and the Making of a Film*, by Deepa's daughter Devyani Saltzman.

ROSA PARKS (1913–2005) was a cleric at the time of her arrest in 1955. A local law or "ordinance" in Montgomery, Alabama, required people of colour to give up their seats to white people. Her refusal to do so and the trial which followed pitted the local law against the US constitutional guarantee of equal rights for all people. While the trial proceeded protesters refused to ride the buses, choosing to walk instead. This boycott almost bankrupted the bus company. After 381 days, the Supreme Court struck down the local law segregating buses on the grounds that it was unconstitutional. Rosa Parks' courage and dignity are credited with sparking off the civil rights movement in the United States.

SAPPHO (*c.* 630–570 BC) was a poet in ancient Greece, famous for her love poems. Perhaps because she was a woman and perhaps because she was reputed to be gay, her works were frequently censored, burned and banned. After two thousand years they were lost entirely and she was only remembered because of references to her in other writers' works. But over the past hundred years, archaeologists combing through ancient garbage heaps have unearthed numerous love letters from antiquity which quote portions of her work. As more and more of these are found, her long-lost poems are gradually being reassembled. Lesbos is the name of the island where Sappho lived.

MY MOTHER AND FATHER came to Canada from England in 1955. My father was a sailor in the British Navy and later a shipper in a factory. My mother worked as a secretary and comedian and also wrote poetry. They are both retired now and live in Scarborough.

As a performer of his own poetry and songs, *ROBERT PRIEST* has been delighting children and their parents for twenty-five years. Robert has also written and performed segments for *Sesame Street*, and *Eric's World*. His play, *Minibugs and Microchips*, received a Chalmers Canadian Play Award for the theatre for young audiences category. Robert lives in Toronto where he is writing his second children's novel, *The Paper Sword*.

JOAN KRYGSMAN is a visual artist and writer from Dundas, Ontario, where she lives with her six-year-old daughter, Fritha. Trained at the Ontario College of Art and Design, Joan works in acrylic, ink, collage and pixels. Along with regular gallery shows, her designs are showcased in children's books, annual festivals across Ontario, and on her website, www.stripedaardvark.com.